Canned cow — evaporated milk

Chicago — pineapple sundae

Chokies — artichokes

C. J. White — cream cheese and jelly sandwich
on white bread

Cow paste — butter

Dough well done with cow to cover —
buttered toast

Drag one through Georgia — Coca-Cola with
chocolate syrup

Flop two — two fried eggs, turned over

Frog sticks — French-fried potatoes

Fry two, let the sun shine — fry two eggs with
yolks unbroken

Georgia pie — peach pie

Guess water — soup

Hen fruit — egg

Hoboken special — pineapple soda with
chocolate ice cream

Hope — oatmeal

# FRANK AND ERNEST

# FRANK AND ERNEST

by Alexandra Day

SCHOLASTIC HARDCOVER

SCHOLASTIC INC.　New York

Library of Congress Cataloging-in-Publication Data

Day, Alexandra.
Frank and Ernest / by Alexandra Day.
p.    cm.
Summary: An elephant and a bear take over a diner and find out
about responsibility and food language.

ISBN 0-590-41557-3

[1. Elephants — Fiction.    2. Bears — Fiction.    3. Restaurants, lunch
rooms, etc. — Fiction.    4. Responsibility — Fiction.]    I. Title.
PZ7.D32915Fr 1988
[E] — dc 19
88–1966
CIP
AC

12  11  10  9  8  7  6  5                    0  1  2  3/9

10

First Scholastic printing, September 1988

"I'll only be gone three days, but my diner is very important to me. I hope you can handle it."

"Don't worry, Mrs. Miller. We will take as good care of it as you would."

"Look here, Ernest. Diners have a language of their own, and we will need to learn it before we can wait on people."

"It's really beautiful, Frank. It will be great fun doing this job, but I think it will also be a huge challenge."

"I'll take a hamburger with lettuce, tomato, and an onion."

"Hey, Frank, burn one,
take it through the garden,
and pin a rose on it."

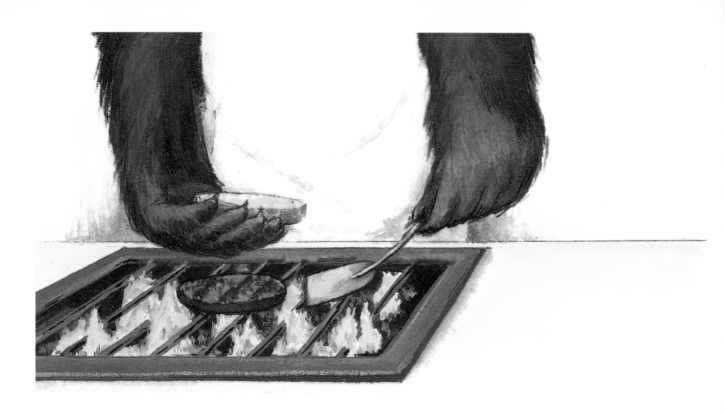

"I'd like a piece
of apple pie and
a glass of milk, please."

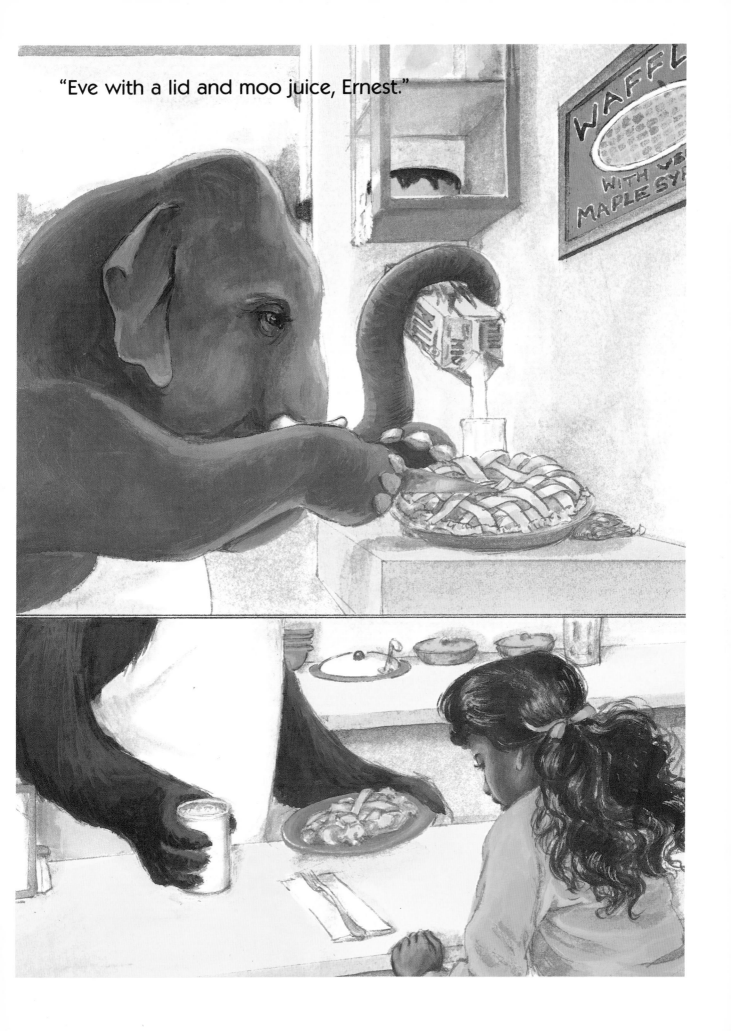

"Eve with a lid and moo juice, Ernest."

"A hot dog with ketchup
for Jimmy, and a serving
of Jell-O for me,
if you please."

"Paint a bow-wow red, Frank,
and I need a nervous pudding."

"Well, Ernest, we made it through the first day."

"Gimme a vanilla milk shake with an egg in it, to go."

"Would you give me a hand, Ernest? I need a white cow — make it cackle and let it walk."

"I'll take the pancakes with maple syrup, and coffee with cream and sugar."

"A stack with Vermont
and a blonde with sand."

"I think we're getting better at this, Ernest."

"May I have an English muffin with butter, and a cup of black coffee, please?"

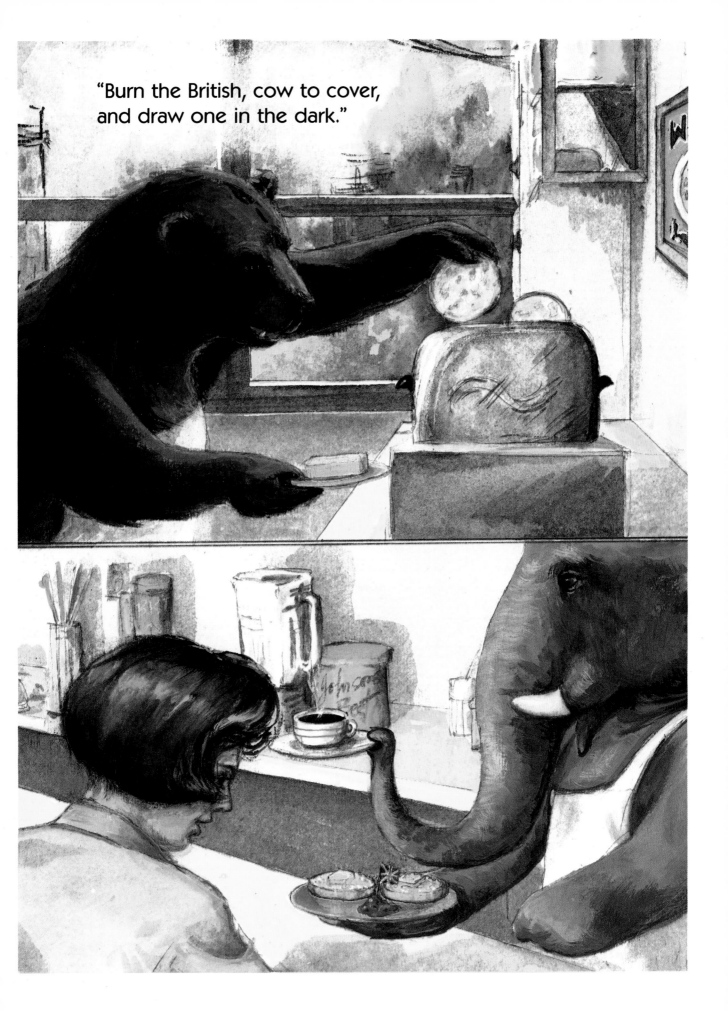

"Burn the British, cow to cover,
and draw one in the dark."

"A tuna sandwich on toast, please,
and a Dr. Pepper with the ice left out."

"Ernest, I need a radio sandwich
down, and an M.D.,
hold the hail."

"I'd like two scrambled eggs on toast, and a cup of tea with lemon, please."

"Adam and Eve on a raft, wreck'em, and a spot with a twist."

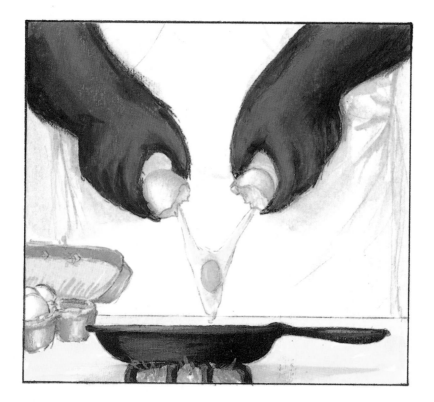

"Well, we did it!"

"Gentlemen, the place looks beautiful, and I've heard nothing but good things from my friends who ate here in the last few days. You did a fine job, and I'll recommend your services to everyone I know."

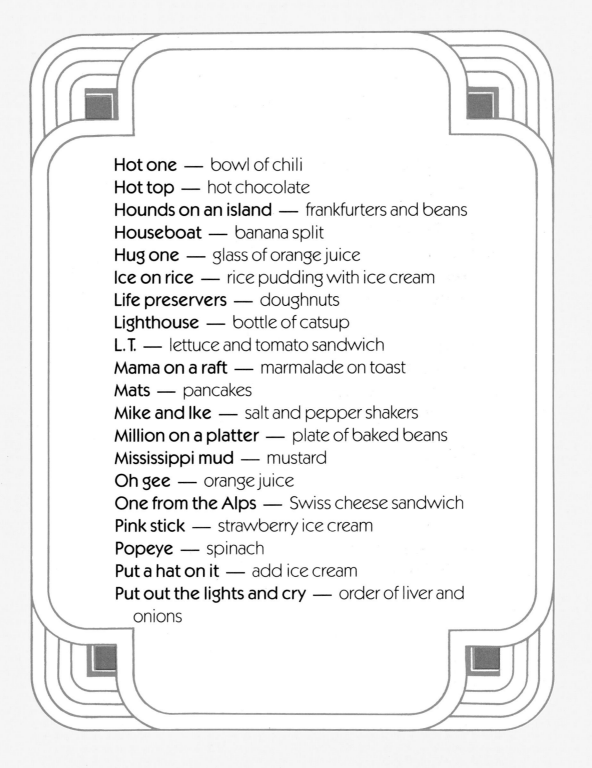

**Hot one** — bowl of chili

**Hot top** — hot chocolate

**Hounds on an island** — frankfurters and beans

**Houseboat** — banana split

**Hug one** — glass of orange juice

**Ice on rice** — rice pudding with ice cream

**Life preservers** — doughnuts

**Lighthouse** — bottle of catsup

**L.T.** — lettuce and tomato sandwich

**Mama on a raft** — marmalade on toast

**Mats** — pancakes

**Mike and Ike** — salt and pepper shakers

**Million on a platter** — plate of baked beans

**Mississippi mud** — mustard

**Oh gee** — orange juice

**One from the Alps** — Swiss cheese sandwich

**Pink stick** — strawberry ice cream

**Popeye** — spinach

**Put a hat on it** — add ice cream

**Put out the lights and cry** — order of liver and onions